this book belongs to:

_____

_____

_____

_____

for

cameron

LITTLE TIGER PRESS
1 The Coda Centre, 189 Munster Road, London SW6 6AW
This paperback edition published 2000
First published in Great Britain 1999
Copyright © 1999 Amanda Leslie
All rights reserved
Amanda Leslie has asserted her rights to be identified
as the author and illustrator of this work under the
Copyright, Designs and Patents Act, 1988
Printed in Malaysia • ISBN 1 85430 699 5
1 3 5 7 9 10 8 6 4 2

Amanda Leslie

flappy waggy wiggly

LITTLE TIGER PRESS
London

who h
wag
yello
and a
licky

woof!

as a

gy

w tail

sticky

tongue?

dog

who h
wrin
green
and
of t

a s a
kly
body
a lot
eeth?

odile

snap!

trumpet!

who a w grey and flappy

has
avy
trunk
big
ears?

who

fluffy

tail fe

and

quacky

has blue

others a

beak?

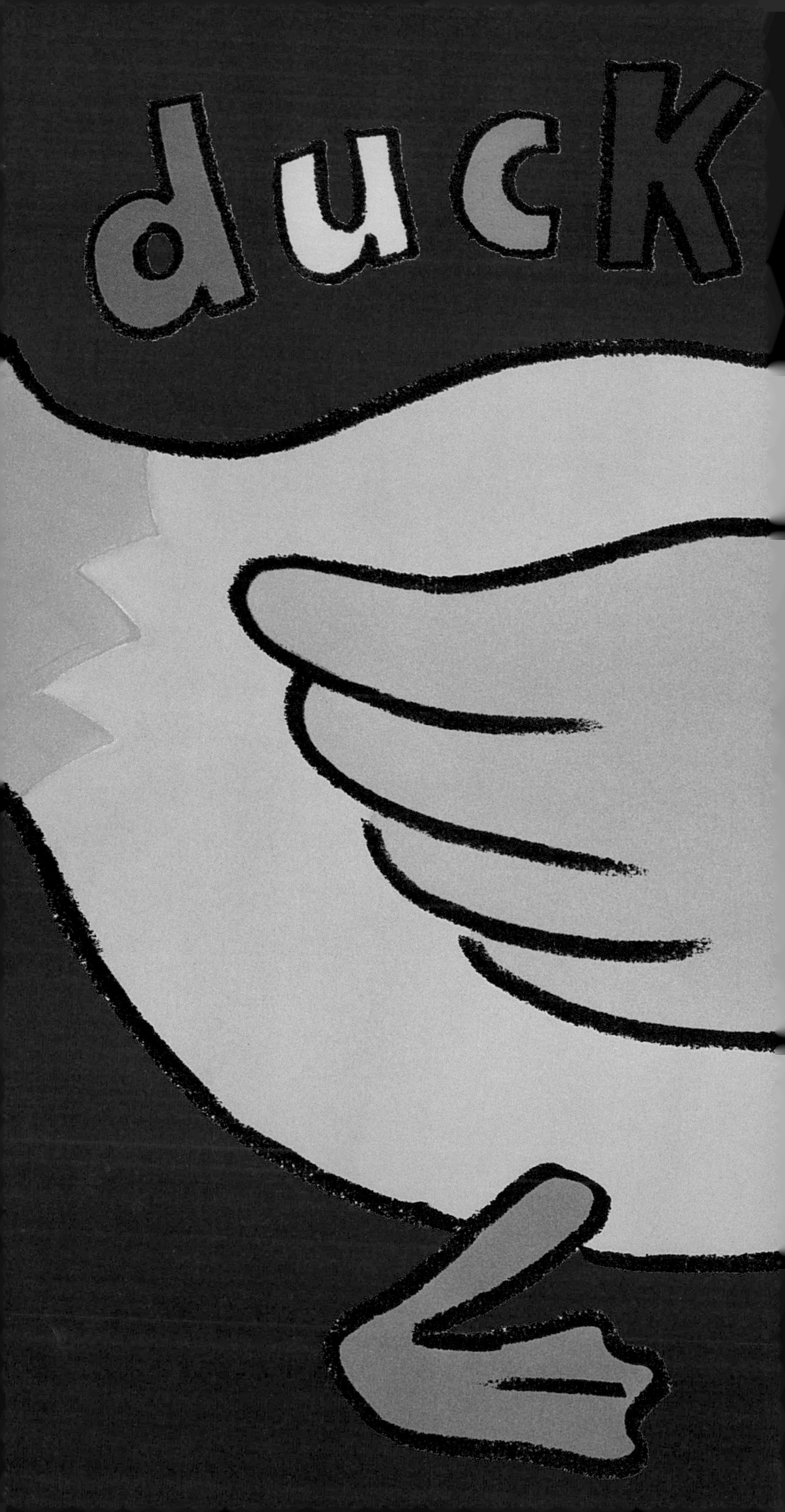
duck

oink!

who h
snuf
pink
an
curly
ta

as a
fly
snout
d a
whirly
il?

who h
long
tongue
spo
sli t
bo

as a a
red d
and a
tty
hery
dy?

hissss!

grrrowl!

a s a

ipy

e tail

big

kers?

ti

oink!

hissss!

trumpet!

snap!

who h
fiddly
ten w
toes
make
these

as ten
fingers
iggly
and
s all
noises?

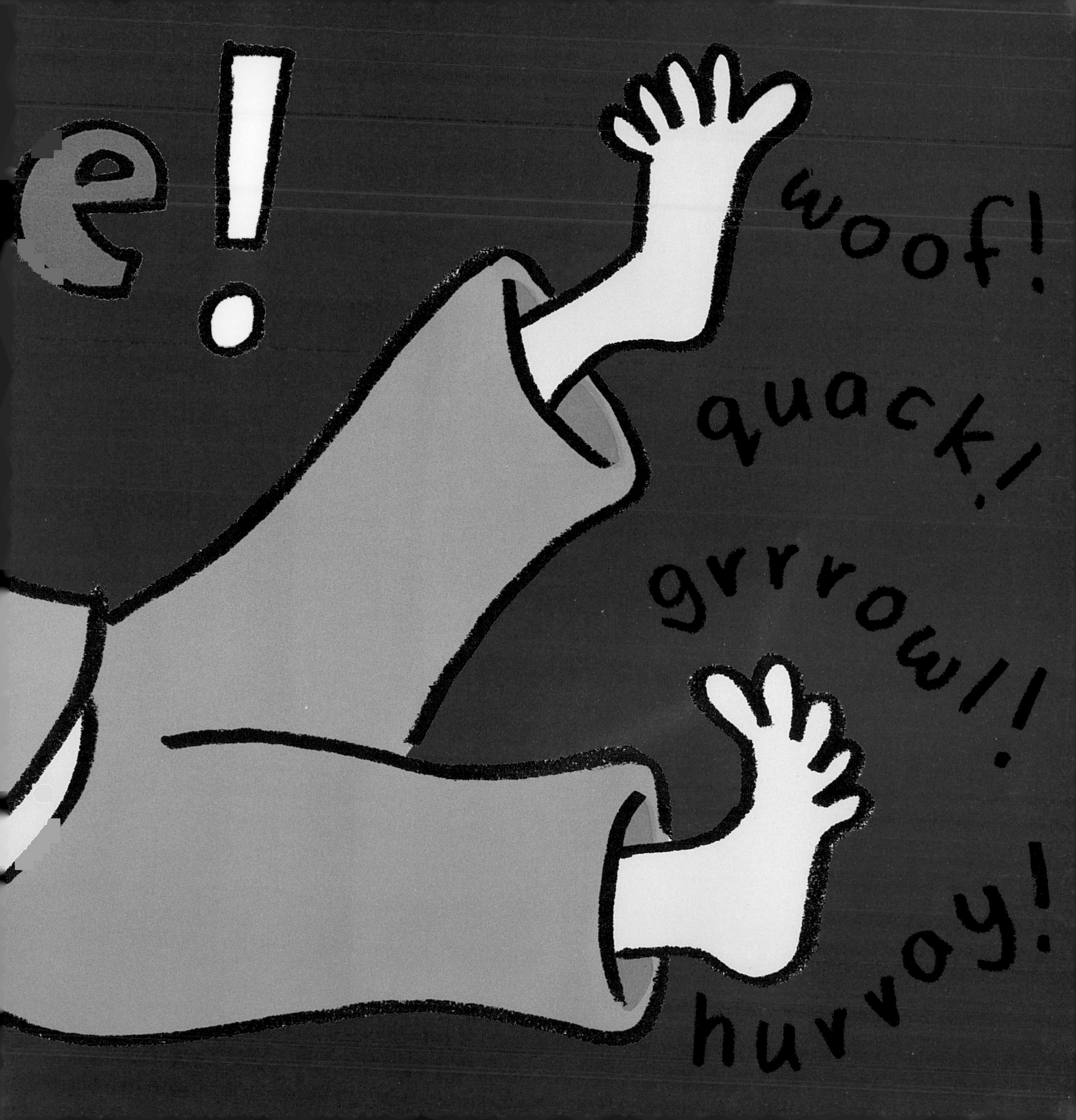
e!
woof!
quack!
grrrowl!
hurray!

and the fun continues...

Goodnight
PiggyWiggy

a pull-the-page book

Christyan and Diane Fox

Titus's
Troublesome
Tooth

LINDA JENNINGS AND
GWYNETH WILLIAMSON

Little Bear's
Grandad

Nigel Gray
Vanessa Cabban

do crocodiles
moo?

A lift-the-flap book

Amanda Leslie

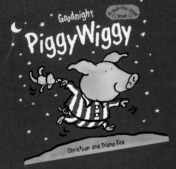

It's my turn!

David Bedford
Elaine Field

Michael Coleman
Tim Warnes

George & Sylvia

A Tale of True Love

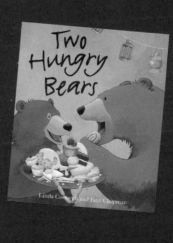

Two
Hungry
Bears

Linda Cornwell and Jane Chapman

Little
Mouse
and the
Big Red Apple

A.H.Benjamin and Gwyneth Williamson

For information regarding any of our titles, or for our
catalogue, please contact us at: Little Tiger Press
1 The Coda Centre, 189 Munster Road, London SW6 6AW
Tel: 020 7385 6333 Fax: 020 7385 7333
email: info@littletiger.co.uk

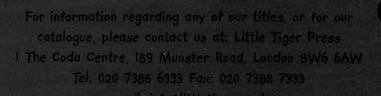